Adiós, Tricycle

Susan Middleton Elya

illustrated by **Elisabeth Schlossberg**

G. P. PUTNAM'S SONS

To my BFF, Joan Van Horn. Sorry about your red crayon. —S.M.E.

For my little ones, Laurent, Claire and Anna.
And for Bernadette, and her not-so-little ones,
Louise, Marion, and Emma. —E.S.

G. P. PUTNAM'S SONS
A division of Penguin Young Readers Group.
Published by The Penguin Group.
Penguin Group (USA) Inc., 375 Hudson Street, New York, NY 10014, U.S.A.
Penguin Group (Canada), 90 Eglinton Avenue East, Suite 700, Toronto, Ontario M4P 2Y3, Canada
(a division of Pearson Penguin Canada Inc.).
Penguin Books Ltd, 80 Strand, London WC2R 0RL, England.
Penguin Ireland, 25 St. Stephen's Green, Dublin 2, Ireland (a division of Penguin Books Ltd.).
Penguin Group (Australia), 250 Camberwell Road, Camberwell, Victoria 3124, Australia
(a division of Pearson Australia Group Pty Ltd).
Penguin Books India Pvt Ltd, 11 Community Centre, Panchsheel Park, New Delhi – 110 017, India.
Penguin Group (NZ), 67 Apollo Drive, Rosedale, North Shore 0632, New Zealand
(a division of Pearson New Zealand Ltd).
Penguin Books (South Africa) (Pty) Ltd, 24 Sturdee Avenue, Rosebank, Johannesburg 2196, South Africa.
Penguin Books Ltd, Registered Offices: 80 Strand, London WC2R 0RL, England.

Manufactured in China by South China Printing Co. Ltd.
Design by Ryan Thomann.
Text set in ITC Highlander.
The art was done with pastels on colored paper.

Library of Congress Cataloging-in-Publication Data
Elya, Susan Middleton, 1955–
Adiós, tricycle / Susan Middleton Elya ; illustrated by Elisabeth Schlossberg. p. cm.
Summary: Even though he has outgrown his tricycle, a boy hides it at his family's
yard sale until just the right smaller child comes along. Includes glossary of Spanish words used.
[1. Stories in rhyme. 2. Growth—Fiction. 3. Bicycles and bicycling—Fiction.
4. Garage sales—Fiction.] I. Schlossberg, Elisabeth, ill. II. Title.
PZ8.3.E514Ad 2009 [E]—dc22 2008006562
ISBN 978-0-399-24522-0
10 9 8 7 6 5 4 3 2 1

Yard is filled with outgrown **ropa**,
pots for **plantas**, bowls for **sopa**,

curtains made of corduroy,
this old trike—my favorite toy.

It's too small because I'm growing.
Look, my belly button's showing.

Riding used to be a breeze.
Now, instead, I bump my knees.

¡Oye! Hear the screech of tires.
It's the early-morning buyers.

They swoop down to buy our things.
Someone tries the bell. It rings.

My old trike is too appealing.
Coast is clear, so I start wheeling.

Sneak past **Papi** and **Mamá**,
hide it by our old **sofá**.

What a sale—it's one big **venta**!
Count the money—**cuenta**, **cuenta**.

A dime, a quarter, look at that!
A buck for **Papi**'s dusty hat.

Mothers buy my small **camisas**.
Our old things bring smiles—**sonrisas**.

Sell our treasures, sell our junk.
Take **monedas**. Hear them plunk!

Near the baskets, someone's stalking,
sees my trike, so I start talking.

"How about this map of France?"
Nope, he buys a pair of pants.

Crowds keep coming—bustle, bustle.
Papi lifts the couch with muscle.

Now I see some handlebars,
so I stack the canning jars.

Still my trike's a red-hot item.
If they want to buy, I'll fight 'em.

Make two fists is what I do.
Buyer walks right past it. Phew!

Sun shines higher—**brilla, brilla**.
Sit down in a shady **silla**.

Things picked over, table bare.
¡Ay! Now someone buys the chair!

Crowds are gone now, **Papi** sweeping,
says the rest is not worth keeping,

stacks the rejects by the wall,
great big pile for us to haul.

My **triciclo** looks so lonely.
"It'd be nice," says Dad, "if only

someone little came on by,
gave that shiny ride a try."

Hold it! **Un señor** is stopping,
here to do last-minute shopping.

Then his **hija** makes a dash,
grabs my trike. "We'll pay in cash."

I am **grande**, she is smaller.
She is **baja**, I am taller.

When she looks me in the eye,
time to tell my trike good-bye.

Papi says to count **dinero**.
Will there be enough? **¡Espero!**

At the toy store, run inside.
Smile upon my face, this wide.

Shake the cash box, jingle, jingle.
Then I see it, feel a tingle.

Venta finished—now **completa**,
it just bought **mi bicicleta**!

Glossary and Pronunciation Guide

adiós (ah DYOCE) good-bye

ay (I) oh

baja (BAH hah) short

bicicleta (bee see KLEH tah) bicycle

brilla (BREE yah) it shines

camisas (kah MEE sahs) shirts

completa (kome PLEH tah) completed

cuenta (KWEHN tah) count

dinero (dee NEH roe) money

espero (ehs PEH roe) I hope

grande (GRAHN deh) big

hija (EE hah) daughter

Mamá (mah MAH) Mom

mi (MEE) my

monedas (moe NEH dahs) coins

oye (OE yeh) listen

Papi (PAH pee) Daddy

plantas (PLAHN tahs) plants

ropa (RROE pah) clothing

silla (SEE yah) chair

sonrisas (sone REE sahs) smiles

sofá (soe FAH) sofa

sopa (SOE pah) soup

triciclo (tree SEE kloe) tricycle

un señor (OON seh NYOHR) a man

venta (VEHN tah) sale